"Excuse me, I'm looking for a unicorn! Have you seen one anywhere?"

"**YOO-HOO!** Unicorn! Is that you by that tree?"

"No, not me! I'm just a bear doing bear things.

RAWR!

Can't you see?"

"I want to ride a unicorn!
But I have to look far and wide.

"AHA!
There's one!"

"Who me? No way!
I'm a wild zebra with a stripey hide."

"There must be a unicorn farm where the sign says to go."

"Oh, yes! It's true.
Just head on down that road!"

"Please say you're a unicorn!
Or else I'm really sunk."

"Pardon me, you kind of look like a unicorn. Do you think we could go for a ride?"

"Would a unicorn cluck like this,
and peck from side to side?"

"I just **HAVE** to ride a unicorn.
Why does it have to be this hard?"

"If I could ride a unicorn,
I'd be the **QUEEN** of the world!
If I could ride a unicorn,
my whole heart would **TWiRL**.

"If I could ride a unicorn
Everyone would think I'm neat.
If I could ride a unicorn,
I'd always land on my feet."

"Hey! I'm pretty sure
these are unicorn tracks!
And I definitely saw a tail.

"I simply must find
that beautiful creature.
I really don't want to fail."

"I'm determined to ride a unicorn,
Then everyone will be my friend.

"**AHA!** There it is!
Right around that bend!"

"Being a unicorn means I'm extra special,
That's what people always say.

"But what if my sparkles dim,
or my magic fades away?"

"I want to be loved for who I am,
And not just my colorful mane.
I want people to know what's inside my heart—
Not all unicorns are the same!"

"I'd love to be your friend,
And get to know you more."

"Being the **TRUEST** you
is what friendships are for!"

"We don't have to prove a thing to anybody else."